THE MYSTERY ARTIST

written by Pleasant DeSpain

illustrated by Mel Crawford

To Paul Thompson, for believing in me from the beginning

Published by Riverbank Press
801 94th Avenue North, St. Petersburg, Florida 33702

Copyright © 1996 by Riverbank Press, a division of PAGES, Inc.

Printed in the United States of America

2   4   6   8   10   9   7   5   3   1

I S B N   0 - 8 7 4 0 6 - 7 7 3 - 1

How THE MYSTERY ARTIST came to be

This is the first story I ever made up and wrote down. It happened a very long time ago, when I was in the third grade. My best friend was named Ricky, and he couldn't find a single story with his name in it. Ricky knew that I liked to make up stories, and he asked me to write one just for him. We didn't have Young Authors, or even journal writing in school, when I was a boy. But Ricky was my friend and I didn't want to let him down.

That night, I wrote the entire story. I drew pictures and colored them in, and made a book cover out of cardboard. I must admit that I wasn't nearly as good an artist as the Little Ricky in the story.

I lived one block from school and ran all the way to class the next morning. Ricky wanted to read the story right away. Our teacher, Mrs. Hanson, said it was time for math. Ricky's desk was right behind mine, and he started hitting me on the back. Ouch! I slipped him the book.

He read it and whispered, "Great story, Pleasant. Thanks."

Mrs. Hanson heard him and walked back toward us. She took the book away and saw my name on the cover. (I should have been like Little Ricky and not signed it.) She said, "You know better than to disturb class, Pleasant. Go to the front of the room and read your story out loud."

I was scared, and my voice shook, but I read my story. Guess what happened? The class liked it!

Mrs. Hanson liked it, too. She said if I kept on using my imagination and writing my stories down, I might grow up to be an author. And that's just what happened.

—*Pleasant DeSpain*

A little boy mouse
named Ricky lived in
a large mouse village,
not so very long ago.

Little Ricky loved to draw and to color and to paint. Each time he finished a new picture, he wrote his name in the bottom right-hand corner, like a real artist.

One day, Ricky's teacher asked everyone to draw a picture of the outdoors, with mountains and trees and a summer sky.

What would you put in the empty sky? A golden sun? Some fluffy white clouds? A few high-flying birds?

That's what all the other mice drew. But not Little Ricky.

He saw the world a bit differently and filled his sky with the most wonderful things he could possibly imagine.

Instead of birds, Ricky drew five flying tennis shoes. Then he colored them purple! Rather than a bright sun, he put in a gigantic upside-down alarm clock with time running backwards! In place of soft clouds, Ricky painted a green kangaroo hopping up and down!

"Drawing time is over," said the teacher. "Put your names on your pictures, and I'll tape them to the wall. Then we can see everybody's good work."

Little Ricky put his name in the bottom right-hand corner and handed in his picture.

His teacher said, "Ricky, yours is different from everyone else's, but I'll put it up with the others."

All the mice-kids looked at Ricky's picture and said, "Yuck! It's all wrong! Ricky's not a good artist."

That hurt. Little Ricky loved to draw and color and paint.
He decided not to show his pictures to anyone else.
He put a sign on his bedroom door that said
STAY OUT!

Every day after school, Ricky ran home and closed his door and made his pictures the way he wanted to. Only now, when he finished one, he didn't sign his name in the lower right-hand corner. He left it blank.

Three months went by, and Little Ricky had seventeen wonderful, terrific, and pretty good paintings in his closet. He liked them a lot, but he was sad.

"I wish I could show them to everyone at school," he said, "but they would just laugh."

Suddenly, he had a brilliant idea!

Early the next morning, with everyone else in his family still asleep, Ricky sneaked all of his pictures into the garage and piled them into his red wagon. He tied the wagon's long handle to the back of his bike and pedaled all the way to the center of the mouse village.

He stopped at the
museum and pushed
on the big front door.
It was locked.

So he slipped his unsigned
pictures under the museum
door, one by one.

Then, as fast as the wind, he rode his bike back home, pulling the empty wagon behind.

Ricky tip-toed back to his bed, crawled in, and closed his eyes.

It wasn't long before his mom peeked into his room and said, "Time to get up, dear. I'm fixing your favorite breakfast, chocolate pancakes!"

Just as Ricky sat down to eat, the mice who ran the museum arrived downtown and unlocked the heavy front door. They gasped at the seventeen strange pictures scattered all over the floor!

The museum mice lined the pictures up against
a long wall and took a careful look.

Finally, they agreed. "These are wonderful!"
they exclaimed. "So imaginative, so fun, so alive!"

"But they are not signed," one mouse said.
"Who painted them? Who is the artist?
We must find out!"

The museum mice called the local newspaper,
and a reporter came over and took photographs.

The next day, Ricky's paintings were on the front page of the mouse paper, along with a question in big bold letters: **WHO IS THE MYSTERY ARTIST?**

Little Ricky admitted that he had painted the pictures. The museum mice put a beautiful frame around each one and hung them on the walls for everyone to see. Ricky was so happy that he signed all seventeen in the lower right-hand corner.

Ricky's entire school went to the museum on a special field trip, just to see his artwork. Ever since that day, his teacher and all his classmates agree that Little Ricky is a wonderful artist!

About the Author

Pleasant DeSpain

Pleasant DeSpain got his name from his great-great-grandfather, his great-grandfather, his grandfather, and his uncle. He is the fifth-generation Pleasant in his family.

Recognized as a pioneer in American storytelling, Pleasant is a former university instructor, television host, and newspaper columnist. The mayor proclaimed him "Seattle's Resident Storyteller" in 1975.

Pleasant appears at major storytelling festivals throughout the country and gives programs in schools each year. He also teaches Young Author workshops and encourages children everywhere to use their imaginations.

He is the author of *Twenty-Two Splendid Tales to Tell*, Volumes 1 & 2, *Thirty-Three Multicultural Tales to Tell*, *Eleven Turtle Tales*, and *Strongheart Jack and the Beanstalk*. He also creates computer story-games. When asked why he tells stories, Pleasant says, "We are all natural storytellers. Our lives are our stories. When we share our stories, we come alive!"

About the Illustrator

Mel Crawford

Growing up in Canada, Mel Crawford always wanted to be an artist. During World War II, he served in the Canadian Navy. He then used his veteran's benefits to attend the Royal Ontario College of Art.

After graduation, he came to the United States, where he found work with the *New York Times* and the *Weekly Reader*, the television program *Sesame Street*, and several publishing houses.

Widely acclaimed as a painter and illustrator, Mel has exhibited his work throughout North America. His work can be found in museums and in homes of private collectors. Mel has twice been a finalist in the Arts For The Parks competition. In 1994 he won third prize in the Wyoming Conservation Stamp Art competition.

He has lived in Connecticut for more than thirty years.